JB's HARMONICA

John Sebastian

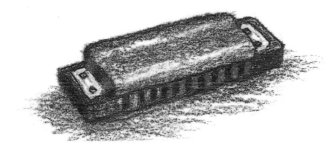

Illustrated by Garth Williams

HARCOURT BRACE JOVANOVICH, PUBLISHERS

San Diego   New York   London

Text copyright © 1993 by John Sebastian
Illustrations copyright © 1993 by Garth Williams

Library of Congress Cataloging-in-Publication Data
Sebastian, John, 1944–
J. B.'s harmonica /John Sebastian; illustrated by Garth Williams —
1st ed.
p.   cm.
Summary: After continually being compared to his father, a famous
harmonica player, J. B. decides not to play his harmonica anymore until he
realizes that he can be a musician and be himself, too.
ISBN 0-15-240091-5
[1. Harmonica — Fiction. 2. Musicians — Fiction. 3. Identity — Fiction.
4. Fathers and sons — Fiction.] I. Williams, Garth, ill.
II. Title.
PZ7.S4428Jb   1993
[E] — dc20   91-35841

First edition
A B C D E

The display type was set in Spire.
The text type was set in Cochin.
Color separations were made by Bright Arts, Ltd., Singapore.
Printed and bound by Tien Wah Press, Singapore
Production supervision by Warren Wallerstein and Ginger Boyer
Designed by Lisa Peters

The inspiration for this story came from
Jane Bishir Sebastian and John Sebastian, my
parents, who created the original
"J. B.'s Happy Harmonica," a children's album.

This book is dedicated to them.

Special thanks to Bonnie Verburg and Allyn Johnston,
without whom this book might not have happened,
to Ben and John Charles, who have always
been my best audience, and to
Catherine for help in
the 11th hour.

— *J. S.*

With love to my wife, Leticia.

— *G. W.*

JAMES BEAR had a lot on his mind as he headed home from Bearsville school. Tomorrow was the day his father would bring home the new harmonicas, and J. B. was impatient for tomorrow to come.

He ran up the steps of his house to the familiar sounds of his mother's typewriter and his father practicing the harmonica.

As evening came, his father's practicing
mixed with the city noise and made a lullaby for
J. B. while his mother told him a good-night
story and tucked him into bed.

Next morning, the new harmonicas arrived just as they had for as long as J. B. could remember. His father filled the house with music as he tried out each one.

But this year was different. This year, Father gave J. B. a special harmonica just for him.

J. B. tootled while his father practiced. He puffed and blew and pretended he was playing a concert at Bearnegie Hall just like his father.

After lots of puffing and blowing and pretending, an amazing thing began to happen.

Every now and then, in the middle of the funny noises, a little tune came out. The more J. B. pretended to play, the more the noises sounded like music.

Sometimes it seemed the harmonica was magic. But J. B.'s dad knew what was happening.

"The more you play an instrument, the more you can play the sounds in your head," he said. "There's music in everybody. Practicing just makes you better at letting it out."

J. B. practiced more and more. He played in the schoolyard after lunch, and he played at home before he went to sleep. He played during parties his parents had, and soon people began to say, "You're getting good, J. B. When you grow up, maybe you'll play the harmonica just like your dad."

At first, J. B. liked people saying nice things. But the more it happened, the more something about it bothered him.

J. B. didn't know *what* he would be when he grew up. Maybe he'd rather be an archaeologist and search for dinosaur bones.

Or maybe he'd rather be a veterinarian who played harmonica for his patients. He loved his dad, but he knew he might like to be something very different.

So J. B. decided he wouldn't play his harmonica anymore.

And he didn't. At least until his mom had a party for all of her writer friends.

The writers always tried to make each other laugh with stories they made up. One writer told a story using one of J. B.'s puppets, and everybody laughed. Without thinking, J. B. picked up his harmonica and played funny music to go along with the story.

When the music and the story ended together, everyone roared with laughter.

"That's great, J. B.," laughed Earl, the biggest and loudest of the writers. "You're getting as good as your dad on that harmonica."

J. B. stopped playing and left the room. Only his mom noticed that he was angry.

When the party was over, she asked him about it.

"Why do people want to compare me with Dad?" asked J. B.

Mom sat down at her thinking place in front of the typewriter. "If you hit the target with your toy bow and arrow and I called you Robin Hood, would that be all right?"

J. B. nodded grumpily.

"And if you baked bread and I said it was like Mrs. Zito's, would that be okay?"

J. B. tried to keep a straight face, but even thinking about Mrs. Zito's bread made him smile.

"It's a way of saying you're good — comparing you to someone good. I know it's a little different when it's your dad, but don't let that make you feel bad about something you do so well."

J. B. thought about that all during breakfast the next day. He thought it over all through recess at school. He thought about it all the way home.

He was still thinking about it after dinner when his father said, "You know, J. B., I miss that little tune you used to tootle when I practiced."

J. B. was quiet for a moment. Then he said, "Well, Dad, when I play in front of people, they say I'm going to be just like you when I grow up. And I don't know — do you want me to be just like you?"

His dad smiled and sat down next to J. B.

"Remember when I said that there's music in everybody? Well, it's true. All of us have our very own song inside. Your song is your own. Sometimes people say silly things to tell you they like your playing, but nobody really wants you to be just like me."

"I guess my song is the one that slips out sometimes when I play on the stoop," said J. B.

"I've heard that song," said his dad. "That's the one I've been missing!"

J. B. smiled, picked up the harmonica, and played
the little tune while his father's eyes twinkled.

"Your very own song," said Dad.

"My very own song," said J. B.

Then J. B. really surprised his dad. He played the
song he always heard when he was going to sleep, one
of his father's songs.

But he played it his very own way.

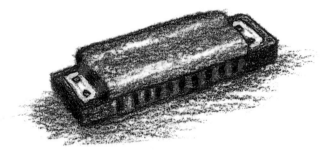